The Things They Saw:

A Collection of Short Stories

By Neal McNeil

ISBN-10: 1508836531

ISBN-13: 978-1508836537

To my family.

Contents

The Tomorrow Dream

I've had the dreams for as long as I can remember. I thought I was normal. I thought everyone had the Tomorrow Dream. That is, until the morning of my eleventh birthday. That Friday morning, in a disoriented panic, I rushed out of bed and downstairs into the kitchen. I stood in front of my mother, my cheeks streaked with tears. Her gaze was concentrated on the contents of the mixing bowl that she held against her stomach. One hand gripped the bowl; the other held a large wooden spoon.

"Cassandra. Breakfast's not ready yet. What are you doing up so early?" When she raised her head and saw the tears in my eyes the spoon fell from her hand and rattled on the linoleum floor.

I remember the anguished look on her face. The despair of a mother seeing her child in pain. For a moment, looking at her, I forgot my own sorrow and what had made me rush to her for comfort.

"What is it, baby? What's wrong?" She bent down and cupped my face in her hands, wiping my tears away as her eyes began to fill with tears of her own.

"It's . . . Rex!" I forced the words out between sobbing gasps. "He got out of the fence. A car. He's gone!" I let the weight of my body fall into my mother's arms, my body trembling as I cried. My mother stroked my hair and wiped tears from both of our eyes.

"No, no, baby. Rex is just fine. You must have had a bad dream." She looked into my eyes and gave me a reassuring smile. "I know he's gotten out a few times this week but, look." She took my hand and led me to the kitchen window. "He's right there," she said, pointing at our black, white, and brown English Foxhound.

She continued trying to calm me. She spoke in a hushed voice with a smile on her face. "Your dad is going to fix the fence today so that he can't get out again. Everything is going to be okay sweetie." She walked me to the kitchen table where we sat and talked more.

Through my slowing tears I explained to my mother that it was not an ordinary dream that I had about Rex. "No, Mom, it wasn't a regular dream. It was the Tomorrow Dream! He's gonna get hit by a car today!"

My mother was stunned. That's when I saw it in her face. That was the moment that I realized she didn't have any idea of what I was talking about. Maybe she did not have the dreams. Maybe I was the only one who had the dreams. As she consoled me, I began to doubt myself. Had I ever really had a dream that foretold the future? Perhaps my vivid imagination and poor memory combined to confuse me, making me think that I had foreseen the future. That is what I wanted to believe. So that is what I would try to convinced myself for the rest of the day. It was all in my imagination.

I ate my waffles in silence.

My class threw a birthday party for me during lunch. Actually, it wasn't a party just for me. It was a party to celebrate the last day of school. But, because the last day of school happened to be on my birthday, I told myself that the party was for me. We all ate pizza and my mother brought two large birthday cakes to share with the class.

The food and festivities did little to ease my worries. My mind raced all day. Was it just a dream? I know that I had had the Tomorrow Dream many times before, and I thought that the dream always came true. Now, I began to doubt that reality. Sometimes I couldn't remember the Tomorrow Dream fully. I would wake up in the middle of the night and just know that I had had a special dream. The next day, I would have a déjà vu experience. My young mind reasoned that the déjà vu was simply my dream coming true, even though I couldn't remember exactly what that dream was.

My mother stayed at school with me after lunch. She organized a few activities for the class while my teacher began storing supplies that she would use next school year. I kept a forced smile on my face as my mother led us through group games. In the back of my mind I continued to worry about Rex.

The ride home from school was quiet. I sat in the passenger seat of my mom's car dreading our arrival at home. I wished the ride would last forever. That we would never get home to face the news about Rex.

My mother parked the car in our driveway. I noticed several planks of wood lying in the grass. My dad had obviously been to the lumber yard and was preparing to repair our fence. It didn't look like he had gotten started yet. The fence still had its loose, broken planks pushed aside forming a perfect escape portal for Rex.

There was a handwritten note on the kitchen counter waiting for us. My mother picked it up. As she read to herself, her brow furrowed. She turned to me and reached out for my hand.

In a soft voice she said to me, "Honey, your dad is at the veterinarian's office. Rex was in an accident."

Tears puddled in my eyes. I couldn't think straight. I only had one question for my mother. "Why didn't you believe me?"

That day removed all doubts that my Tomorrow Dream was real. It was also a clarifying moment. I understood that not only was my dream real, but also that no one would believe me if I told them about it.

* * *

The dreams continued as I grew older. Sometimes they were vague. When I would wake, I couldn't be sure that I had even had a dream. But during the day, I would have that eerie feeling of déjà vu. However, sometimes the dream would be vivid. Every detail of my surroundings would be crystal clear. I would hear other people's conversations if I happened to be in a public place. I could smell dinner cooking if I were in a kitchen. Even in dreams that I didn't have sensory input, I could still feel emotions. Happiness, sadness, anger, fear.

During these years I analyzed every aspect of the Tomorrow Dream. I came to understand that it didn't show me some random event that would happen the next day. No. It was specific. It showed me my life as it would be at some time between 3:30 PM and 4:30 PM the next day. I don't know why. That's just the way it worked. It didn't matter what time zone I would be in. The timing of the Tomorrow Dream was consistent.

I tried to capitalize on my precognitive abilities, but I never could. As a starving undergrad at Penn, I organized a weekend day trip to Atlantic City with a few friends. My plan was to make sure that I was at the Roulette table from

3:30 to 4:30 the next afternoon. With every drop of the ball, I would check my watch to see the time. If all went well, I would be able to double the little bit of money that I had.

All did not go well. In my dream the night before the trip, I saw the Roulette fall into the Black 24 slot. I looked at my watch – 4:07 PM. I didn't see any other spins of the wheel in my dream, but that was ok.

The next morning on the way to Atlantic City a multiple car accident brought traffic to a standstill. We waited on the highway for what had to be hours before we were able to continue. By the time I got to the roulette table it was exactly 4:07 PM. I watched the ball land on Black 24.

Maybe my gift could not be used for my personal gain. I learned to accept the dream as just a part of who I was. I ignored them for the most part, and continued my life as best I could.

* * *

The terrorist attack happened on a Wednesday, just a few minutes after 10 am. A dirty bomb exploded at the base of the Lincoln Memorial. The explosion killed four tourists and a National Parks Service Ranger. Five others were seriously injured, and dozens of tourists were showered with large doses of radioactive material.

The explosive device itself was not extremely powerful. Those killed or injured were all within about ten feet of the child-sized book bag that contained the bomb. Radioactive material rained down on visitors within about a fifty foot radius. The light July breeze scattered more radioactive dust eastward over the reflecting pool and the Vietnam and Korean War memorials.

Public outrage was instant and unprecedented. The immediate death toll was nowhere near the toll of the attacks of 9/11. But this time, the terrorists killed more than just American citizens. This time, the terrorists killed part of America itself. The Lincoln Memorial, the Reflecting Pool, and the Vietnam and Korean War memorials might never be able to be visited again. Constitution Gardens and the World War II memorial could be cleaned, but it would be a generation, or two before visitors would be allowed on those grounds again.

I dreamt of the National Mall attack the night before is happened. In the Tomorrow Dream, I sat staring at a special news report of the blast. The reporter didn't have much information yet. Only that there was an explosion, multiple deaths, and radioactive fallout. Eye witnesses placed ground zero of the explosion somewhere between the steps of the Lincoln Memorial and the edge of the Reflecting Pool.

As soon as I awoke from the dream I began making calls. I called the FBI, CIA, DC Metro Police, Park Police, Secret Service, and even the NSA. Someone had to listen! All my life, this gift has been a curse. To see the future but to be powerless to have anyone believe me. I thought that this, this was, at last, the reason why I was gifted (or cursed), to stop this atrocity that was about to be committed.

The law enforcement agencies didn't take my calls seriously. The bomb exploded at 10:10 am, July 9, 2019. Everything I saw in the dream came true, and worse. Months after the attack, it was revealed that radiation poisoning had sickened nearly two hundred citizens. Many of them would die slow and painful deaths. Also, the powers-that-be determined that a portion of our nation's capital, from the Lincoln Monument to the World War II

Memorial would be walled off forever, encased in concrete five feet thick. A sarcophagus for America's dead land.

I was arrested within a day of the attack. Telephone records led the authorities to my doorstep. Of course no one believed the truth, that the Tomorrow Dream predicted the attack.

* * *

I ate waffles for breakfast today. My execution is scheduled for noon. Because of the highly-charged anti-terrorism climate, my trial was rushed to court and the discharge of my sentence expedited. Not quite four years have passed between my arrest and today's scheduled execution. I quickly exhausted all of my appeals. The only thing that can stop the execution now is a pardon from the President.

In my years of incarceration, I have become an international celebrity. Psychic followers and skeptics alike have used me as a poster child for their causes. Depending on whom you ask, I'm either the second-coming of Nostradamus, or a cautionary tale of charlatans and the gullible public who idolize them.

However, the furor raised by the psychic community was nothing compared to the worldwide religious community. In those circles, I have been called both history's worst blasphemer and its greatest prophet. Some have written me letters asking for me to use my final words before execution to describe the after-life. Think of the billions of souls you could save if you made the world believe! Some have written to ask that I not say anything. Only through faith can a soul enter the Kingdom of Heaven. And then there are those who declare that I am just a fraud. Do not listen to what the prophets are prophesying to you; they fill you with false hopes. They speak visions from their own minds, not from the mouth of the Lord.

I slept soundly last night. Did I have the Tomorrow Dream? Did I have a vision of what I will see between 3:30 and 4:30 today? Did I see Heaven, Hell, nothing? Or, maybe I saw a pardon in my future. The world is waiting for an answer. But I'm not going to tell them if I saw anything. What's the point? They wouldn't believe me anyway. They never have.

The whirring of the generator subsided. Dr. Granger let a smile slip across his face. He wasn't quite sure if he had succeeded. He was still in the classified ward of the research laboratory, but something was different. The fluorescent lights overhead flashed on and off intermittently, throwing long shadows on the walls and floors, momentarily confusing his eyes.

Granger released the restraining harness and stepped out of the machine. He could feel heat radiating from the generator. The machine was much hotter than he had expected. In the flickering light, the steady red glow of a wall-mounted digital clock caught his eye. 8:48 PM. The clock displayed the date underneath the time. November 11, 2086. He had succeeded. The doctor laughed heartily with the knowledge that he was now the first man to pick a specific moment in time and instantaneously travel to that very moment. His name would undoubtedly be written in every history book to come. Who knows, he may even drop in to a history class a hundred years in the future to chat with the kids who are studying him.

Granger stepped slowly out of the room and into the hallway. None of the overhead lights seemed to be working. His path was illuminated by dim orange foot-level emergency lighting. The low lighting did not bother him. He had walked this maze of hallways to his office for years. He could walk it in complete darkness if he needed to.

The massive four-story facility was built in the shape of an equilateral triangle with sides over 1700 feet in length. The building contained nearly five million square feet of office, research, and retail space, making it one of the largest office buildings in the world. Each floor of the building was laid in a grid formation, similar to that of a city's downtown area. Hallways, with a few exceptions, ran parallel and perpendicular, creating large city blocks on which individual offices and laboratories were located. The "Incircle Hallway" circled the interior of the triangular building. Retail shops, eateries, and vending machines were located at various locations on the first floor Incircle. A huge open reception area occupied the front corner of the triangle.

In the hallway outside of the test room, Granger bumped a metal trashcan, tipping it onto the floor. The contents rattled inside as the can rolled down the hallway. The sound echoed into the cavernous lobby. Granger paused. He heard a barely audible voice calling out in the darkness.

"Conrad! Come out of the shadows and face me like a man!" He recognized the voice. It was his own voice, coming from another part of the building.

Granger hurried his pace to a slow jog. He did not enter the reception area, but instead, turned down an intersecting hallway leading towards his office. When Granger was at the door of his office he heard the voice again. It was still far away. But now it was moving.

"What? Did you think you could just push me aside and claim responsibility for my work? You want the fame and glory without the blood, sweat, and tears?"

A second voice echoed through the halls, "Conrad?"

Granger sprinted towards the second voice. He ran as fast as his business Oxford shoes would permit. Crossing halls. Turning corners. As he ran past yet another intersection, plaster from the corridor wall flew into his face. Only after he wiped the dust from his forehead did he realize that he had heard gunfire. Someone's shooting at me! A rush of adrenaline surged through his veins.

Granger had once joked that, to the unfamiliar, the crisscrossed interconnecting hallways in this facility could be more difficult to navigate than any labyrinth an ancient Greek god could design. The only thing missing in this building, he said, was a blood hungry Minotaur hunting down its unsuspecting prey. Now, he wondered if that Minotaur was lurking at last. A Minotaur with a gun. A Minotaur named Conrad.

Granger quickly searched his mind for an alternate route back to the containment room. More plaster kicked him in the face. As he rounded a corner he approached a dark figure standing in the hall. He yelled as he darted past the shadowy figured. "Hide!"

Granger was well down the hallway before he realized that the person he had just passed was himself.

Rounding another corner, he was finally back at the containment room and the safety of the time machine. Pausing for a second, he wondered if his future self had heeded the advice and gotten out of harm's way.

In the distance, a muted yell rang out, "No! Wait!"

Two gunshots echoed in the halls. Silence.

Dr. Granger opened the containment room door and pulled the handle on a fire alarm inside. As the sirens wailed, he sprinted towards the time machine, inserted a key, and rapidly tapped buttons. The machine whirred back to life. In the blink of an eye the containment room was brightly lit. He searched the walls for the clock. It read 8:50 PM, August 15, 2086.

* * *

A bead of sweat swelled on Dr. Granger's temple. As its size increased, it lost grip of the clean-shaven skin. Rolling down Granger's cheek and onto his chin, the drop let go of his face, finally coming to rest on a desktop calendar. His breath came in rushes and pants. His chest ached as the lungs beneath attempted to fill beyond their capacities. The room wobbled beneath him. His vision blurred.

Granger didn't know how long he had been sitting behind his desk. He did not even realize that he was behind the desk at all. His mind was elsewhere, replaying the events that had just taken place. Or were they events that will take place? His hands trembled as he searched his pockets for a key to unlock a file cabinet next to his desk. He retrieved a folder labelled "Project 31 (File #60)" and set it down. Inside of the folder, a memo, dated a week earlier, lay on top of dozens of other papers.

TOP SECRET – EYES ONLY

To: Dr. Claudius Granger

From: Dr. Ralph Conrad, Acting Director, SGP

Date: 8/07/86

Re: Project 31

Dr. Granger:

It has come to my attention that some accounting department staff have begun to question the budget requests for Project 31. I remind you that all requests for funds should be directed to me. At this late date in the development cycle, we cannot afford any unnecessary scrutiny of our work. Project 31 is listed as a prototype flight simulator in our accounting books. Any expenditure made through official channels should reflect such.

I will be visiting the laboratory in the evening on Monday, November 11. Your last update indicated that you were prepared to proceed with test travels. I would like a demonstration during my visit. Also, please have a copy of the operations manual printed for me to take back to Washington.

I have arranged for the building to be cleared on the day of the visit. Most employees will be out for the Veteran's Day holiday. The remaining skeleton staff will be excused. We will be able to proceed with the test without disturbance or interference.

Regards,

Dr. Ralph P. Conrad

Granger read a portion of the memo again. ". . . we cannot afford any unnecessary scrutiny of our work." *We*? *Our* work? Who the hell does Conrad think he is? An attention-seeking, ladder-climbing, self-righteous suit from DC! Granger took a deep breath trying to compose himself.

Granger had mistrusted Dr. Conrad from the very moment the two first met face-to-face one year ago. He believed that Dr. Conrad was not truly interested in the groundbreaking work going on at the facility. He assumed that his new supervisor was only interested in the accolades and promotion potential that a successful project would bring.

We. *Our* work. Conrad had only visited the facility twice in the last year. Now, with success so close at hand, he conveniently plans an inspection. Granger banged a clenched fist on his desk. He knew that Conrad had to have an agenda of his own. He would probably come to town offering a "promotion" with a reassignment out of the Special Government Projects group. Any such reassignment would mean that Conrad would be able to assume responsibility for the ultimate success of the project.

We! *Our* work! Dr. Granger moved a pile of papers in his desk drawer. He removed a wooden box, placed it on the desktop, and took out a handgun. Walking to the containment room, to the time machine, Granger's heart began racing faster and his breaths became short and shallow.

"You're not going to take this away from me, Conrad!"

* * *

Granger adjusted the time machine's controls to take him forward to the moments preceding his earlier trip. The machine came to life. After several seconds, the generator was quiet again. The containment room was brightly lit. Unsure if he had succeeded, Granger searched the wall for the clock. 8:40 PM, November 11. He was back in the future.

Granger climbed out of the machine and looked up at the fluorescent lights. He knew this building like the back of his hand. He could outmaneuver Dr. Conrad easily in the dark. He pulled the gun from his waistband, took aim, and fired one shot. The overhead lights blinked off and then flashed intermittently, throwing long shadows on the walls and floors, momentarily confusing his eyes.

Granger left the containment room. Turning left, he walked towards the end of the hall. He opened a steel door and entered the Mechanical Room. Inside, he opened an electrical panel and closed all of the circuit breakers in sight. The overhead lights in the building went black. In the hallways, foot-level orange emergency lights flickered to life.

He followed the orange lighting towards the front entrance of the building. Granger drew the gun from his waistband again. If Conrad was already waiting, Granger would be ready for him. He moved cautiously towards the entrance.

The atrium was even darker than the hallways. There was no emergency lighting in this area, only reflective striping along the floor baseboards and two illuminated overhead EXIT signs. Granger sat on a sofa near the front door, the waiting area for guests. He realized that he was breathing heavily again; his heart racing.

Granger took deep breaths to calm himself. This was not the kind of person he was working to become. He had let emotions get the best of him again. Two years of anger management counseling had been negated in just a few hours. Why had he come back to this time to confront Conrad? Would it not be more rational to inform the police that Conrad is going to try to kill him? Probably not. How would that conversation proceed? "I'm telling the truth officer! I went to the future and my boss is going to try to kill me!" The insane asylum would have a new resident within minutes.

The sound of metal rattling in a darkened hallway shook Granger out of his contemplative state. The anger that had begun to subside, welled up again. He stood and pointed the gun into the darkness.

"Conrad! Come out of the shadows and face me like a man!"

He moved slowly towards the hallway from which the noise emanated. His pulse quickened. Trepidation and anger muddled his thinking. He had lost control of his emotions, again. He saw a shadow moving along the darkened corridor.

Granger yelled into the darkness. "What? Did you think you could just push me aside and claim responsibility for my work? You want the fame and glory without the blood, sweat, and tears?"

He was no more that forty yards away from the figure in the hall when Granger heard a voice coming from a different area of the building. "Conrad?"

The shadowy figure began to run and turned into an intersecting hallway leading in the direction of the voice. Granger ran to the closest intersecting hallway and turned into it. He was now on a parallel path, albeit several blocks away. If he was fast enough, he would be able to catch the figure before it could do any harm to Granger's other self.

Granger came to an intersection in the hallway. He caught a glimpse of the figure crossing the same intersection further down the corridor. He instinctively raised the gun and fired. He heard the bullet slam into the plaster wall far in the distance, but he did not hear Conrad cry out in pain. The prick must have dodged the bullet.

Granger ran down the corridor until he reached the intersecting hallway where his target was. He saw the man fleeing. Now only about twenty yards separated the two. He raised the gun and fired another shoot. Plaster fell from a wall. The sound of the gunshot echoed throughout the building. The figure turned left into another hallway. He had missed again.

Granger gave chase, sprinting in the footsteps of his prey. He turned into the same hallway as the man he was chasing. Granger stopped in his tracks. At the far end of the corridor, the figure stood facing him. The figure spoke but Granger could not make out the words. His attention was focused on the man's arms. As the figure spoke, it raised its hands. It was holding something. Granger fired two shots into the man's chest.

Alarm bells rang loudly. Granger turned and re-traced his path, running as quickly as possible through the darkened hallways. He reached the containment room, inserted his key into the time machine, and started the process. The machine came to life. In the blink of an eye the containment room was brightly lit. He searched the walls for the clock. It read 9:27 PM, August 15, 2086.

* * *

Dr. Granger found himself sitting behind his desk again. He was practicing the relaxation techniques that his therapist had taught him. Breathe in. Count to five. Breathe out. Count to five. Repeat. The exercise seemed to be working.

After a few minutes he stopped the breathing exercises and started progressive muscle relaxation. He flexed his toes in his shoes. He held the flexed position for about ten seconds and then released. Next, he raised his toes off of the floor so that only his heels were grounded. He flexed the soleus and tibialis anterior in each leg. Hold ten seconds. Granger continued flexing muscle groups in this manner, from toe to head, until he finished with his eyelids. Close tight. Hold ten seconds. Open. Now, he was relaxed.

* * *

It had been nearly three months since the day Granger had taken the time machine for a test run. Nearly three months since the day that he believed he shot Conrad. In reality, that day was still one week away, but Granger had been obsessing about the events for the last eighty-one days.

Is it possible to change the future? Are the events that he witnessed destined to happen? When explaining time travel, Granger often liked to make the analogy that the flow of time was like the three states of matter in which water exists. The past, in his example, would be a solid, like ice. It has a constant shape and volume. The past, being a solid, is unchangeable. Hence, travel to the past is impossible.

The present is liquid. Like the past, it is tangible, but unlike the past, the present can be manipulated and shaped to conform to our desires. Just as one can dig irrigation channels and change the course of a river, one can also influence the flow of the present and change the course of history.

The future, in Granger's analogy, was a gas, like steam. The gaseous future has no definite shape, volume, or pressure. But, with careful effort, one can affect the form of the future.

Reflecting on this analogy, he concluded that the events that he witnessed during the journeys into the future did not have to happen. Indeed, none of what he witnessed on November 11 would happen if he could prevent Conrad from visiting the facility.

The ding of his email notification jarred him from his deep thoughts. The notification box flashed red and white indicating that a high-priority, encrypted message had arrived. He read the notification box and his heart began beating faster.

From: Ralph P. Conrad

Subject: November 11 Visit

Priority: HIGH

Granger backed himself from his desk, walked to his office door and closed it, and returned to his chair. He opened the email. There was a document attached. He clicked the icon and opened the file. He felt tension leave his muscles as he read the message. It seemed as if his problems were solved.

TOP SECRET – EYES ONLY

To: Dr. Claudius Granger

From: Dr. Ralph Conrad, Acting Director, SGP

Date: 11/04/86

Re: Project 31

Dr. Granger:

I hope the day finds you well. I have good news for you. I had hoped to keep the purpose of my November 11 visit secret. However, because of security issues, and scheduling conflicts, you need to be aware of the real motivation for my coming to the facility.

The President is aware of the research you are conducting. I have passed along all of the updates you have given me. He is excited about the project and would like to meet you personally.

Because of other appearances that the President is obligated to make for the Veteran's Day holiday on November 11, we will need to postpone our visit until the following week.

I am sorry for the inconvenience. I will send you an updated schedule as soon as possible.

Congratulations and Regards,

Dr. Ralph P. Conrad

TOP SECRET – EYES ONLY

* * *

November 11, 2086, 8:35 PM. The facility was dark and quiet. The Veteran's Day holiday plus Dr. Conrad's decree to give all personnel the day off ensured that the only activity at the building was several security guards patrolling the outside grounds.

The President's visit had been rescheduled to November 28, another holiday on which Conrad would ensure that the building was completely empty. Because Dr. Conrad had rescheduled his visit, Granger felt assured that the future he had traveled into would not occur. Granger arrived at the office at 8:00 PM. This would be his last week working the night shift. The events he experienced two months ago forced him to reexamine his life and get serious about resolving the lingering anger and interpersonal relations issues which had originally caused him to seek the aid of a therapist. Granger increased his therapy visits to five per week. Now, after three months of the daily sessions, his doctor told him that it was time to integrate back into the society which he had shunned for nearly a year. He had decided that on the following Monday, he would come into the office at 8:00 AM like most of his peers.

Granger sat behind his desk, feverishly typing, making final edits to the time machine user manual. After nearly an hour, it was time for a break. He left his office and walked to the vending machines that lined the Incircle hallway. He slid a five dollar bill into one of the machines and pressed a button. He bent down and retrieved his Dr. Pepper. As he was kneeling, the overhead lights in the building shut off. Dim yellow foot-level emergency lighting flickered to life.

He muttered, "This can't be. Conrad's not here. The future has changed."

A figure sprinted past him in the dark. He heard the person yell, "Hide!" But, in shock, he found himself unable to move. Then he saw it – another shadow at the end of the hall.

"No! Wait!" He yelled, raising his hands in the air. He heard two gunshots. Granger's legs buckled beneath him. He collapsed.

Stay-At-Home Mom

10,000 BC. The reed wall cut the light from the rising sun into hundreds of ribbons, painting the floor and the opposite wall of the hut with streaks of yellow. The woman had hoped that she could rest for just a little while longer. Her infant had had a fitful night. It cried, seemingly continually, keeping her from sleeping much. Even now, as she slowly awakened, she heard the child crying once more.

The woman lifted the child up from its bed of leaves. The leaves were stained with the remains of last night's feeding. She held the infant in one hand and gathered the soiled bedding with the other. After tossing the leaves in a pile behind the hut, she heaped new leaves onto the earthen floor.

After feeding the child, she strapped it to her chest using a sling of fur and animal skin. Then, she gathered the pole with water carriers attached at each end. The walk to the river would be long, but she needed to get there before the sun was high in the sky. It was the dry season, and when the sun was high, the heat would be unbearable.

The sun was almost halfway to the top of the sky by the time she arrived at the riverbank. Her progress had been slow because she stopped several times to feed the child and clean the leaves in the sling. Weary from the walk and the lack of sleep, she found a tree to rest against. She set the water carriers and her baby on the ground to her side. Her eyelids became heavy.

The sound of her baby's crying jolted the woman to consciousness. She opened her eyes. Then she saw it - an animal's fury tail disappearing into the tall grass lining the riverbank. Gru-ah! She knew immediately that one of the beasts was attempting to steal her child. Mother gru-ah often gathered live small prey to bring to their cubs. The mothers taught their cubs how to kill and feed in the safety of their own dens.

In one fluid motion, the woman rose and ran after the animal. She lifted the covering of a small pouch she wore around her waist. She sprinted into the grass as she grabbed two disk-shaped stones with sharpened edges out of the pouch.

The gru-ah was about thirty paces ahead of the woman. It trotted slowly, unconcerned. It held the sack containing the crying baby in its front teeth, careful not to apply too much pressure, lest its cubs would be denied the experience of their first kill. The gru-ah did not know that, regardless of how careful it was, her cubs would not get a kill on this day.

The woman hurled one of the sharpened stones at the gru-ah. It hit the animal high on its right rear leg. The gru-ah roared in pain. It dropped the infant and turned to see what had caused the burning in its leg.

The woman stood tall as the gru-ah faced her. The animal bared its large flesh-tearing teeth and began charging. The gru-ah was within ten paces when the second stone hit it in the neck. The animal squealed and stumbled to the ground. It stood and looked at the woman. A small patch of fur near the animal's neck was wet with blood.

The gru-ah took a step towards the woman, growled, and stopped. The woman raised her hand into the air, pretending to hold another rock. The gru-ah took another tentative step forward.

Thirty paces away from the woman, the baby began crying loudly. The gru-ah turned to look at the squirming prey and then looked at the woman. The woman took a step towards the gru-ah and yelled as loudly as her voice would let her. She waved an empty hand above her head, threatening to throw a non-existent stone. The animal looked in the direction of the prey again and back to the woman. The gru-ah lowered its head and sauntered away from the woman and child.

The sun was at the top of the sky by the time the woman had gathered the water. The heat seemed to weigh the stick down even more than the full water carriers. The walk home was long and arduous. She felt dizzy at times. She stopped often to rest and wipe the sweat from her brow. At least the baby slept soundly.

That night in the hut the woman prepared herself for the next day's tasks. She used a twine made of roots to stitch long pieces of wet bark together. In the morning, she would wrap the bark around her lower legs before she entered the woods to gather fruits and berries. The wood coverings would protect her from the bite of a deadly ground slider.

During the last dry season, on a day she had neglected to wear her protection, a ground slider had bitten the woman on the front of her leg. Luckily, she was able to suck most of the poison out with her mouth. Still, she fell terribly ill and was unable to leave her hut for three sunrises. That would never happen again.

As the woman prepared for bed, she thought of her mate. He and the other young men of the village had been away on a hunt for three sunrises. He would be home in four more risings. She always worried so much about him when he was away. Hunting was a very dangerous task, not like collecting water or gathering fruits and berries. She said a chant for his safety.

The woman crawled onto her bed of leaves and closed her eyes. Moonlight glinted through the reed wall. The baby began crying.

Working the Night Shift

It's the second week of summer vacation and I just finished first grade! My mommy says I'm a big girl now. I'm sitting at the kitchen table waiting for Claudia to bring my lunch. My big sister is sitting across from me. She's blowing air through the straw sticking out of her glass of milk. The bubbles make the milk jump out of the glass. She's funny!

Claudia is making peanut butter and jelly sandwiches and the doorbell rings. When she walks to the door, my sister sucks some milk into her straw and spits it out at me. Ewww! She's laughing at me now. I get up and run over to hit her but I hear Claudia yelling something at the front door. She sounds mad.

I hear a loud noise and Claudia stops yelling. I grab my sister's hand because I'm scared and she's two years older than me. She always protects me.

Two big men wearing scary masks come running into the kitchen. I'm holding onto my sister, but they pull us apart. She reaches for me, but one of the mean men hits her in the face and she falls down and doesn't move. I'm crying really loud now. The other mean man picks me up and carries me to the front door. I try to hit and kick him but I can't. When he takes me past the front door I see Claudia lying in red stuff. Her eyes are open but she's not moving.

The mean man takes me outside and puts me in a car. I'm screaming and crying and . . . .

"Dan, wake up!" I heard my wife saying. She was shaking me vigorously. "You were having a nightmare," she said. "You almost punched me in the face!"

I looked at her with a confused expression. I felt afraid. There were tears rolling down my face.

"My god, Dan! Are you alright?" She wiped my face dry with her thumb. "Were you dreaming about a case you're working on?" she asked.

I told her about the dream and that it had nothing to do with my caseload. I wasn't sure where that dream had come from. It was so vivid. It was as if I were being stripped away from my family in reality. Even after talking about it for a few minutes, I was still trembling.

I thought that maybe I had overheard one of the detectives talking about something similar. I told my wife that I would ask around at work. She held me. I slept the rest of the night with no dreams.

I didn't have any luck at the office. I described the dream to my partner but it didn't ring any bells for him. I asked the Shift Sergeant if the scenario sounded familiar. He wasn't aware of any similar home invasion or kidnapping cases either. I put the dream out of my mind and concentrated on the work at hand. Baltimore city gets nearly two hundred murders per year. I'm a homicide detective, a murder police. I needed to concentrate on my real-life, open cases, and not be distracted by an imaginary one.

* * *

I'm in the back seat of a car kicking and screaming. The mean man is sitting beside me holding my arms. I look out of the car window and see a street sign. Ellicott St, NW. I remember that a friend once told me that you can't read in your dreams. Something about the part of the brain that recognizes written words isn't active while you're sleeping. I guess he was wrong.

I take a look at my clothes to see what I'm wearing. A pink t-shirt, pink pajama bottoms, white socks, and no shoes.

I turn to look at the man and ask who he is. He takes his mask off and tells me not to worry. He says my daddy has a lot of money and he will pay to get me home soon. The man has a funny-sounding voice. Like the people that my mommy watches on that boring public TV channel. The man says that if I act bad that I will never go home again. I close my eyes and start crying.

When I open my eyes we're walking up the steps to the front door of a row house. Then I see it. The number on the door is 625. A woman opens the door and says, "Bloody 'ell, Edward! You weren't supposed to bring 'er 'ere!"

I'm inside of the house. A kitty cat is rubbing against my leg. I like kitties. I want my mommy. I start crying again. I look around the room and see . . . .

"Honey! Wake up!" My wife is shaking me awake. "You were crying. Are you sure you're okay?"

I gave her a reassuring smile and told her that I was alright. I told her about the dream and how real it felt. I asked her not to wake me if it happens again because I wanted to know what comes next. She understood. She understood that I'm police. That I needed to know what happens next. We slept soundly until the morning. I didn't dream anymore that night.

* * *

I recognized the format of the street sign from my dream. Ellicott Street NW. That was a Washington, DC sign. Baltimore city doesn't use the directional notation (NW, SW, NE, SE) on our street signs.

When I got into the office, I searched the national crime database to see if I could find any unsolved kidnapping cases from northwest DC. I wasn't really surprised with what I found. The dreams were too detailed, and the feelings were too intense, to just be something out of my imagination. The dreams felt real, and the database results confirmed that they were real.

The crime database indicated that, three years ago in upper northwest Washington, DC, the daughter of a wealthy international banker Charles Stonefellow was kidnapped. During the commission of the crime, the family's nanny, eighteen year old Claudia Radulescu, was killed. The young child was returned four days later, but the murder of Claudia Radulescu was never solved.

I tracked down the detective in charge of investigating the Radulescu murder. That first phone conversation with Detective Richard Hammond was fairly odd. I didn't want to sound like one of those psychic loonies who call me trying to help solve a crime. He listened to me with the same skepticism that I listen to those crackpots who call me. But, because I am one of the boys on blue, I think he let me go on for a little longer than I expected.

Detective Hammond told me that although the investigation has gone cold, he still maintains a relationship with the Stonefellow family. The little girl, Jasmine, was not able to provide any information about her abductors. The doctors said that she had a form of post-traumatic stress syndrome. All memories of the events appeared to be suppressed. She did, however, have terrifying nightmares. She's been re-living those days over and over again. She wakes up terrified, but when she's calmed down, she can't remember what happened in the dreams.

According to Jasmine's parents, she had become a very introverted young girl. The once bubbly personality was now guarded. She was afraid to let anyone get emotionally close to her. The mean men, she thought, would come back some day and hurt all the people she loved. Det. Hammond said that he promised Jasmine that one day he would catch the mean men and no one would ever be able to hurt her or her family again.

Hammond thanked me for calling. He assured me that he would take into consideration all that I had said.

* * *

We are leaving the row house. The funny-talking people are telling me to get into a car. I see a street sign. It says Oak St, NW. Mommy says Oak trees are poison to horses.

We ride for a long time. The woman is in the back seat with me. The mean men are in front. The man that's driving says we're going to the zoo.

I am sitting on a bench near the place where the pandas play. The people left me here a long, long time ago. I'm really scared. A zookeeper comes to talk to me.

I'm in a room eating a candy bar and drinking a soda. I see mommy, daddy, and my big sister come into the room! They run to me and we all hug. Mommy's crying. I'm crying too.

I woke up with a smile on my face. I was crying again, but I knew that these were tears of joy, not terror. I woke my wife and told her what happened. We slept peacefully for the rest of the night.

The next morning called Hammond to relay the additional information I had gathered from the previous night's dream.

* * *

I continued to dream about Jasmine. Some nights I would wake up in a cold sweat. Other nights I would wake up crying. Then, after a month of nightmares, the dreams stopped as abruptly as they began.

A couple of weeks later, Det. Hammond called to tell me that he had closed the case on the Radulescu murder. DC police had arrested Edward Noble, a British national and former employee of Charles Stonefellow's. Edward's sister, Elizabeth, of 625 Oak Street, NW was also apprehended. Cat hairs found in Elizabeth's home matched hairs that the DC forensics department found on Jasmine's pajama bottoms and socks. A second man was being held for questioning in London.

Hammond told me that Jasmine was beginning to open up now that she knew the mean men had been caught. He's seen her smile. She's even given him a hug. Her parents say that she's been sleeping soundly throughout the nights.

I was happy to hear that the case was closed. I never dreamed of little Jasmine again. Eventually, I came to believe that I wasn't really dreaming about Jasmine. I believe that I was dreaming with her, reliving the nightmare with her, over and over again. I believe that I was taking some of the pain of those memories away from her.

I told my wife about Jasmine at dinner that night. We went to bed happy.

* * *

I thank the customer and tell him to come again soon. The next customer in line steps forward and gives me a withdrawal slip. In the 'amount' space he has written 'ALL OF IT.' The man pulls a gun from under his jacket and yells "Everyone on the floor! This thing'll go very easy if you cooperate!"

Also By Neal McNeil

Available in print and e-book versions at Amazon.com:

Scientists, Psychics & Psychotics

About the Author

Neal McNeil has a B.S. in Electrical Engineering from Hampton University. He currently lives in Maryland and works full time as an engineer in Washington, DC, and part-time as an actor in local film, television, and stage productions. Inspired by classic television series such as The Twilight Zone and The Outer Limits, Mr. McNeil's short stories combine science, humor, and drama producing thought-provoking and compelling entertainment.

Made in the USA
Middletown, DE
17 February 2016